THE SHAWNEE

ELAINE LANDAU

THE SHAWNEE

Franklin Watts   *A Division of Grolier Publishing*
New York   London   Hong Kong   Sydney   Danbury, Connecticut
A First Book

Map by Joe LeMonnier
Photographs ©: Ben Klaffke: cover, 3, 8, 11, 21, 25, 26, 32, 35, 56, 57;
Cincinnati Historical Society: 17, 46, 50; Library of Congress: 13, 49;
The Library of Virginia: 40; North Wind Picture Archives: 30, 34, 38, 45, 53;
Northwest Trek Wildlife Park: 19; Ohio Historical Society: 42; The Daily
Oklahoman: 55; Wildlife Park, Eatonville, Washington: 10, 29.

Library of Congress Cataloging-in-Publication Data

Landau, Elaine.
The Shawnee / by Elaine Landau.
p. cm. — (A first book)
Includes bibliographical references and index.
Summary: Describes the history, culture, religion, and traditions of the Shawnee
Indians.
ISBN 0-531-20247-X (lib. bdg.) — ISBN 0-531-15818-7 (pbk).
1. Shawnee Indians—History—Juvenile literature. 2. Shawnee Indians—Social life
and customs—Juvenile literature. [1. Shawnee Indians. 2. Indians of North
America.] I. Title. II. Series.
E99.S35L36 1996
973′.04973—dc20   96-537   CIP
                                                                                        AC

CONTENTS

For Brenna and Jeremy

A RIVER VIEW
FROM SHAWNEE
OKLAHOMA.

THE SHAWNEE

September had just ended. Now the brisk autumn breeze and the trees' golden leaves signaled to the American Indians known as the Shawnee to prepare for the cold winter months ahead. Soon they would leave their village homes. Whole families would set up campsites in valleys where game was plentiful.

The Shawnee would be away from their villages for the entire winter. Therefore, they chose campsites that were somewhat sheltered from the season's harsh winds and snow. Yet, many Shawnee would not remain at these campsites very long. Only children, the elderly, and those too ill to hunt stayed there all winter. Healthy adult Shawnee went off on hunting trips. Some trips lasted just a few days. But other times the hunting parties might be gone for as many as two months.

Until nearly the end of December, Shawnee hunters stalked deer, bison, mountain lions, turkeys, and bears. They used animal calls, special songs, and

DEER WERE AMONG THE LARGER
ANIMALS HUNTED BY THE SHAWNEE.

magical charms to draw the forest's game to them. Before the Indians had guns, they used bows and arrows and clubs to kill game.

During January and February, these American Indians hunted and trapped smaller animals such as beavers, raccoons, and rabbits. These animals were valued for both their meat and their fur pelts. Finally, in March, the Shawnee headed home from their winter campsites.

There was much to be done back at their villages. First the fields had to be prepared for spring planting.

Shawnee fields lay south of the villages. Although grouped together, these were actually separate plots of land owned by different Shawnee families. Nevertheless, the women usually farmed the land together and sometimes the men also helped. Every April they planted several different types of corn as well as squash, beans, and pumpkins.

The women tended the crops during the summer. They also gathered wild plants, fruits, nuts, and berries. Some of the food was eaten fresh; other items were dried and stored for use long after the growing

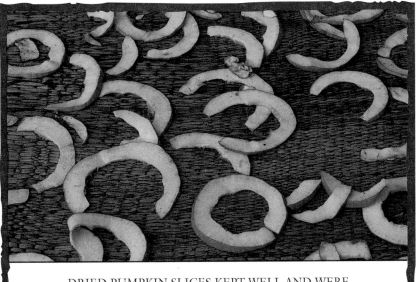

DRIED PUMPKIN SLICES KEPT WELL AND WERE
OFTEN EATEN BY SHAWNEES ON THE MOVE.

season. Shawnee women in the East tapped maple trees in spring for their sap. Further west they drew hickory sap from hickory trees. The men added to the summer food supply by fishing and hunting deer in nearby woods.

Older Shawnee youths helped their parents. Early on these young people learned what was necessary to survive. Even very young children were taught not to yell or cry out because a sudden loud noise could scare game or alert enemies to a family's hiding place. Yet Shawnee parents did not believe in harsh discipline. They did not beat their children. Instead they encouraged young people by praising them for the good things they did.

As they grew older, Shawnee boys learned to hunt and fish alongside their fathers and uncles. Mothers and grandmothers taught Shawnee girls to cook, weave baskets, plant crops, and gather plants for food and medicine. Shawnee women also made and repaired clothing for their families. Shawnee men and boys wore loose shirts, leggings, and moccasins. The females dressed similarly, only their overshirts were usually looser and longer. The women tanned animal hides to make these garments. They also created beautiful bead and ribbon work on outfits worn on special occasions.

NOTICE THE DESIGN WORK ON THE
EARRINGS AND CLOTHING OF A
SHAWNEE MAN IN THIS 1796 PAINTING.

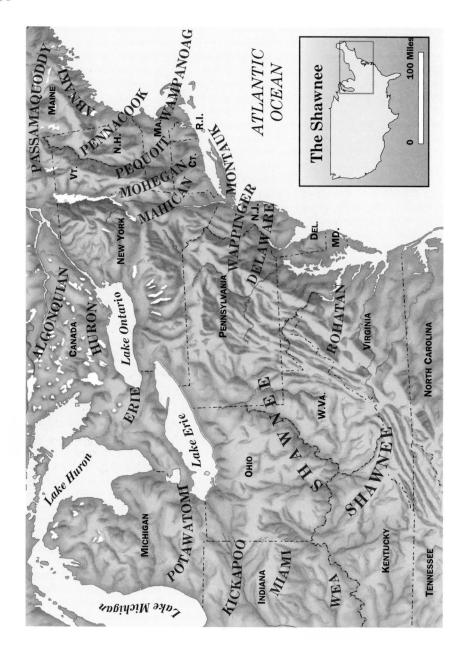

The Shawnee

0   100 Miles

ATLANTIC OCEAN

PASSAMAQUODDY
ABNAKI
MAINE
PENNACOOK
N.H.
VT.
PEQUOTL
MA.
R.I.
MOHEGAN CT.
WAMPANOAG
MAHICAN
MONTAUK
NEW YORK
WAPPINGER
N.J.
DELAWARE
DEL.
MD.
ALGONQUIN
CANADA
HURON
Lake Ontario
PENNSYLVANIA
ROHATAN
ERIE
VIRGINIA
Lake Erie
SHAWNEE
W.VA.
NORTH CAROLINA
Lake Huron
OHIO
SHAWNEE
POTAWATOMI
MICHIGAN
KICKAPOO
MIAMI
WEA
KENTUCKY
Lake Michigan
INDIANA
TENNESSEE

Following a large corn harvest at the end of August, the Shawnee once again prepared to leave for their winter campsites. Being on the move was not uncommon for them. In early times, the Shawnee were a widely scattered American Indian tribe. During the seventeenth century, small Shawnee groups could be found in Illinois, Maryland, and on the Ohio and Savannah rivers. As time passed, they settled into eastern Pennsylvania and continued to move westward. Although some Shawnee settled in Alabama, by the second half of the eighteenth century, most of the tribe lived in southern Ohio. But they would not remain there.

During the American Revolution, and in the years afterwards, groups of Shawnee traveled west across the Mississippi River. In more recent times, they have lived in Oklahoma. Yet despite these changes, the Shawnee never lost sight of their culture and identity as a people. Their story unfolds on these pages.

LIVING SHAWNEE

Throughout the spring, summer, and early fall, the Shawnee lived in their villages. Each village contained a large wooden council house called a *msikamelwi*. Msikamelwis were built of logs, and in some villages might be large enough to hold more than 250 people. In many ways the council house served as a community center of sorts. Celebrations as well as important tribal rituals were performed there.

Surrounding the msikamelwi were the Shawnee's homes. These were smaller round or rectangular structures called *wegiwas*. The wegiwa's frame was made of slender wooden poles driven into the ground and fastened together. Tree bark or animal skins were used to cover it. Spreading animal skins on the ground also made sleeping in the wegiwa more comfortable.

As time passed, Shawnee housing styles changed. Towards the end of the eighteenth century, many Shawnee lived in one-room homes made of logs, boards, or shingles. Most of these structures still had tree-bark roofs.

CLOSEKNIT FAMILIES AND VILLAGES
PROVIDED THE SHAWNEES WITH A
SENSE OF KINSHIP AND COMMUNITY.

Shawnee society was made up of five divisions. When the Shawnee lived in one area, the names of the different divisions may have been taken from closely grouped villages. In any case, these divisions worked together for the tribe's general good. Each was responsible for specific duties.

The two most important divisions—the cha-laakaatha and thawikila—took charge of the tribe's political affairs. The chief of all the Shawnee always came from one of these groups. The other groups performed vital tasks as well. The pekowi division oversaw rituals and ceremonies. These undertakings were a meaningful part of the Shawnee's ancient beliefs and way of life. Members of the mekoche division were responsible for medicine and healing, while the kishpoko division dealt with wartime conflicts.

Each of the various villages also had lesser chiefs. Within Shawnee villages there was usually both a peace chief and a war chief. Among other duties, a peace chief oversaw rituals and celebrations. Often his son became chief when he died.

War chiefs, however, did not inherit their positions. These Shawnee fighters had to show skill and bravery in battle. Before becoming a war chief, a Shawnee was required to lead several successful raids.

There were also female Shawnee chiefs. Often these were the daughters, mothers, or widows of male chiefs. Female peace chiefs oversaw the annual crop planting and special feasts. A female peace chief could also ask a war chief to stop an upcoming raid she did not approve of. These women had the power to spare condemned captives as well. Not all Shawnee females who served as chiefs were peace chiefs, however. Some women fought in battles and became war chiefs.

Within each of the five Shawnee divisions, separate name groups existed. Each of these groups was named for an animal such as the horse, raccoon, rabbit, turtle, or turkey. Members of the various groups often bragged about the animals representing them.

A NUMBER OF ANIMALS INCLUDING THE TURKEY
WERE REPRESENTED IN SHAWNEE NAME GROUPS.

They might also tease other Shawnee about the undesirable traits of their name groups' animals. Yet name groups were taken seriously by these American Indians. A Shawnee's name group was thought to influence that person's fate.

A Shawnee infant's name and the name group he or she would belong to was not solely determined by the child's parents. Instead, two elderly men or women were asked to pray for a name for the baby. The child's parents then picked either of two names suggested by the elderly ones. The names were always from different name groups. This allowed parents to have some say about their child's name group. The baby's name was announced at a naming ceremony held ten days after its birth. Parents invited their friends and relatives to this special feast.

In some cases, a Shawnee changed his or her name and name group. This sometimes occurred if the name selected for the individual had already been given to another person. Shawnee might also change their names later in life if they suffered from poor health most of their life or usually fared poorly in battle. It was hoped that the name switch might improve the person's luck.

Marriages and funerals were also important events among the Shawnee. Shawnee marriages were usually arranged by the couple's parents. The proposal came

GIFTS SUCH AS THIS RABBIT SKIN WERE
PRESENTED TO THE BRIDE'S FAMILY WHEN
A MARRIAGE PROPOSAL WAS MADE.

through the would-be groom's mother to the mother of the bride to be. She would bring animal skins
and other gifts to the girl's family when making the
offer. If the young woman's family accepted the pre-
sents, it meant that the couple would marry.

The female members of the bride's family divided the gifts among themselves. Then they would

prepare a delicious feast of vegetables and fruits for a celebration at the groom's home attended by relatives and friends. Following the feast, the young couple were considered husband and wife. Although Shawnee men were permitted to have more than one wife, this rarely occurred.

The practices surrounding Shawnee funerals were more elaborate. When a Shawnee died, his or her friends dressed that person in new clothes. They also dug the grave and brought the corpse to it. In return for their kindness, the deceased's family gave each of them several of the dead person's possessions.

Shawnee were always buried facing west. At the grave site, friends and relatives tossed bits of tobacco on the corpse asking that the deceased's soul not be concerned about those left behind. After the funeral, a feast was given and followed by a twelve-day mourning period.

Surviving spouses of the dead person, however, continued to express their sorrow. They wore the same clothing everyday and did not wear jewelry or face or body paint during the next year. If the deceased was an important, highly regarded member of the village, a special feast was given a year after his or her death. At that time, surviving relatives gave out gifts to those who attended.

RELIGION

The Shawnee believed they were created by a supreme being known as Our Grandmother or the Creator. This gray-haired deity [god] lived in her home in the sky, where the spirits of the dead also went after leaving the earth. Her grandson, called Rounded Side or Cloudy Boy, along with her small dog, were always nearby as well.

Through Our Grandmother, the Shawnees learned the proper way to live. She showed them how to hunt and farm, build their homes, and worship. Her guidance was evident in both their special ceremonies and their daily conduct.

Each of the five Shawnee divisions had sacred packs or bundles known as *mishaami* to protect them. It was believed that Our Grandmother gave these bundles to the Shawnees, although she determined the prayers and rituals surrounding their use. Some individuals also had their own magic bundles for protection.

Our Grandmother was also thought to have bestowed (given) the gifts of prophecy (seeing into the future) and healing to some Shawnees. A *shaman*, as such individuals were called, could either be male or female. They cured the sick and oversaw religious rituals. A shaman was a highly respected member of the community.

The Shawnees held a number of ceremonial dances each year. The Bread Dances were among the most important of these. During the Spring Bread Dance, the Shawnees prayed for abundant crops. The Fall Bread Dance was held to give thanks for a fruitful growing season and to ask that there be ample game in the months ahead.

Preparing for these special feasts was not left to chance. Twelve specially appointed men hunted game for the Bread Dances. The meat was cooked by twelve Shawnee women selected for this task. Usually those chosen for this duty held this honor for life.

Before a Bread Dance began, a ball game was held in which the women played against the men. The losing team had to gather enough firewood to light the feast's cooking fires as well as keep the campfires burning during the dancing afterwards.

Between the Spring and Fall Bread Dances, the Shawnees observed a number of religious celebrations.

LEG ORNAMENTS LIKE
THESE MIGHT BE WORN
DURING CEREMONIAL DANCES.

CORN, A STAPLE IN THE SHAWNEE DIET, WAS AN
IMPORTANT CROP. THE SHAWNEE PLANTED AND
HARVESTED SEVERAL DIFFERENT TYPES OF CORN EACH YEAR.

These included the annual Green Corn Dance that took place every August at the first corn harvest. During the Green Corn Dance, which could last as long as twelve days, the Shawnees gave thanks to Our Grandmother for the harvest. At that time wrongdoers could also be forgiven for their misdeeds.

Shawnee life included a number of other religious ceremonies and rituals. One was a special spiritual journey taken by Shawnee youths known as a *vision quest*. On a vision quest, a boy or girl went off alone into the woods for several days. There the young person fasted (ate nothing) and did not see or speak to anyone until a vision of his or her spirit guide (usually in the form of an animal or bird) appeared to the individual. The Indians believed that someone's spirit guide helped and protected that person throughout life.

THE EUROPEAN'S EXPANSION

Throughout their history, bands of Shawnee have had to leave their homes to seek out new areas. At times, they were driven away by their enemies, the Iroquois Indians. The Iroquois often fought with surrounding American Indian tribes forcing them to pay tribute. But unfortunately, worse conflicts lay ahead for the Shawnee.

The lives of all American Indians were unimaginably changed by the large numbers of Europeans invading what was once strictly Indian territory. The Shawnee were among the Indians drawn into the struggle between England and France to control North America. Both of these powers tried to recruit American Indian allies hoping to gain the upper hand in the conflict. While the Shawnee had no strong loyalty to either side, for the most part, they fought with the French.

This may have been due to how the French approached settling the New World. Unlike the

British, the French were mainly interested in the fur trade. Instead of sending families to farm the land, trappers seeking animal pelts arrived. Whatever settlements sprang up were necessary for the fur trade.

The French traders were not particularly troublesome to the Shawnees. In return for animal skins, they gave the Indians guns and the European goods (cloth, iron cooking pots, utensils, and so on) on which the Shawnees had become increasingly dependent. The Indians were also still free to hunt, fish, and camp on the land as they always had.

EARLY FRENCH TRADERS DID NOT
MINDLESSLY SLAUGHTER THE BUFFALO
AS BRITISH SETTLERS LATER DID.

TAKEN BY SURPRISE ENROUTE TO FORT DUQUESNE,
NUMEROUS BRITISH SOLDIERS WERE WOUNDED AND KILLED
DURING AN AMBUSH STAGED BY FRENCH AND INDIAN FORCES.

Assisted by the Shawnees and other Indian allies, the French did well. They were victorious in 1755 when British General Edward Braddock tried to capture Fort Duquesne in what is now Pittsburgh, Pennsylvania. The British soldiers marched toward the French fort while playing their drums and wearing the bright red coats of their army's uniforms. They were an easy target for the Indians waiting in the woods to ambush them. The Indians fired from behind the trees while keeping close to the ground. Unable to spot their enemy clearly, the confused British soldiers were soon defeated.

The Shawnees as well as other American Indian groups were extremely helpful to the French on numerous occasions. But the British continued to send additional soldiers and supplies to North America to ensure their army's success. And as the British victories mounted, the French lost their grasp on the territory. In 1758, just three years after their defeat at Fort Duquesne, the British successfully captured the fort. By about 1760, they had largely driven the French out, leaving their Indian allies in a difficult position.

At first it seemed as if the Shawnees might not fare badly. While most of these American Indians fought with the French, some bands of Shawnees had sided with the British. Because of their assistance, the

TOMAHAWKS WERE AMONG
THE WEAPONS USED BY THE
SHAWNEES IN BATTLE.

British were willing to work out a less harsh truce
with all the Shawnees. But as it turned out, the
British victory was hardly beneficial to the tribe.

Unlike the French who had been mostly interested in North America's fur resources, the British
demanded much more. Increasing numbers of
European settlers soon arrived. These were not fur
traders, but farmers who cleared the forests to plow
their fields. These were families hoping to build a new
life in a new land. But unfortunately, it was land on
which the Shawnees had lived for years.

The British also dealt more harshly with the Indians than the French had. Aware that the Shawnees and other tribes had become used to European goods, the French provided them with what they needed to survive the winter. The British, however, refused to continue these good-will gestures to the Indians. They only exchanged supplies for fur pelts even in lean hunting seasons.

The Indians' resentment was further fueled by the British's attitude. While the French treated the Indians with respect, the British's contempt for American Indians was obvious. Believing that the Indians were inferior to whites, they often cheated and exploited the American Indians in their dealing with them. It soon became clear to the Shawnees and other Indians that the British were really only interested in taking their land by any means possible.

As time passed, tensions mounted. The Shawnees, along with a number of other tribes west of the Appalachian Mountains realized that they had to unite to save their people and the land. Leaders from a number of midwestern tribes met to plan a rebellion against the whites. In the summer of 1763, led by an Ottawa Indian chief known as Pontiac, the Shawnees, along with other American Indian allies, declared war on the British.

OTTAWA CHIEF PONTIAC URGED SHAWNEE
LEADERS AS WELL AS CHEIFS FROM OTHER
TRIBES TO UNITE AGAINST THE BRITISH.

Despite difficult odds, the Indians fought bravely. The Shawnee war chief Cornstalk successfully raided white settlements for months. Pucksinwah, another outstanding Shawnee leader, struck both homesteads and British forts. Yet this uprising, which came to be known as Pontiac's Rebellion, only lasted until October. The Indians simply could not match the whites' resources in continuing the struggle. And when the French failed to come to their aid, the Indians knew they would be unable to go on.

A truce was called, resulting in an uneasy peace that lasted for about five years. Then the Iroquois

PEACE PIPES FREQUENTLY WERE
SMOKED AFTER REACHING A
TRUCE ENDING HOSTILITIES.

Indians signed the Fort Stanwix Treaty with the British, which indirectly affected the Shawnees. Claiming that they controlled and spoke for all the area Indians, the Iroquois had signed over Shawnee land as well as territory belonging to several other tribes. In return, the British gave them a sizable sum of money. The Iroquois's claims were entirely false and the British knew it. Yet they used this opportunity to take still more Indian land.

Before long, white surveyors and fur trappers invaded Shawnee hunting grounds in Kentucky and the Ohio River valley. Unlike the Shawnees who were careful to preserve game, the newcomers were careless and wasteful. They readily shot animals for sport or for fur pelts. The meat that Shawnee families had long depended on to survive was left out to rot in the forest. These whites were equally casual about American Indian lives. They were quick to shoot any Indian they spotted on what they now thought of as white territory.

Although the Indians had been defeated in Pontiac's Rebellion and no longer had any hope of assistance from the French, the Shawnees again tried to fight back. They raided the campsites of both the trappers and surveyors who had come to map out the region.

Whites found in the area either received a frightening warning from the Shawnees or were killed. At times, whites were taken captive. While some captives were killed, others were adopted by Shawnee families that had lost a family member.

In June 1771, the Shawnees took Marmaduke von Swearington, a seventeen-year-old white boy, captive. The youth was adopted by Pucksinwah, the Shawnee war chief who had distinguished himself in Pontiac's Rebellion. The Indians called Swearington "Blue Jacket" because that's what he was wearing when he was brought to their village.

Blue Jacket took well to Shawnee life. He learned the Indians' language and customs and was well liked by the tribe. Although he had many opportunities to return to his own people, he chose not to. Instead, Blue Jacket rose to a position of leadership among the Shawnees and on many occasions proved himself in battle.

For the most part, however, the Indians and whites remained at odds. The Shawnees' plight sharply worsened in 1774 when Lord Dunmore, the colonial governor of Virginia, began encouraging white settlements on both sides of the Ohio River and droves of whites responded. Any hope for peace was dashed when a group of white frontiersmen from the region brutally murdered thirteen American Indians without cause. Their victims were women and children from the Shawnee and Mingo tribes. Local whites condemned their actions but the guilty whites were never found and punished.

Unable to muster support from other tribes, the Shawnees decided against waging war against the

LORD DUNMORE, THE COLONIAL GOVERNOR OF VIRGINIA, ENCOURAGED FURTHER BRITISH SETTLEMENTS AT THE INDIAN'S EXPENSE.

whites. The victims' relatives, however, rejoined to take the lives of thirteen white settlers in return. Their revenge marked the start of the conflict known as Lord Dunmore's War. Whites eager to claim even more Indian land took full advantage of the situation. Virginia soldiers destroyed an entire Shawnee village and threatened to continue their rampage. Realizing that they couldn't defeat the enemy, the Shawnees agreed to the whites' demands. But they knew that this time peace came at an especially high price. They were forced to accept the terms of the Fort Stanwix Treaty and surrendered their territory south of Ohio.

UNREST

In 1775, the colonies fought for their independence from Great Britain in the American Revolution. The Shawnees knew this was not their struggle and were anxious to stay out of the fray. Nevertheless, before long, they became involved in the hostilities.

After being offered much-needed trade goods in return for their fighting power, some Shawnee bands sided with the British. But other Shawnees were more concerned about still another rush of settlers into their area. These whites had come trying to avoid the conflict further east. Hoping to find a way to live in peace with them, Cornstalk, the Shawnee chief who fought bravely in both Pontiac's Rebellion and Lord Dunmore's War, visited Fort Randolph in Virginia in November 1777. He was accompanied only by his son and another Shawnee.

THIS MONUMENT HONORS
THE SLAIN SHAWNEE
LEADER CORNSTALK.

But Cornstalk was hardly treated as an ambassador from an independent Indian nation. Instead, the fort's commander decided to hold the three American Indians hostage. Unfortunately, while they were at the fort, a mob broke into the jail and killed the Indians.

Fearing the tribe's revenge, Virginia officials promised to find and punish the murderers. Yet, as in the past, this never happened. Instead, the formerly peace-seeking Shawnees allied themselves with the British declaring war against the Americans.

Even after the Americans officially won their independence from Britain in 1783, the fighting between them and the Indians continued. The Shawnees raided settlements in Kentucky and other areas. Their attacks were often swift and successful. Some were led by Blue Jacket, the white who had been adopted by the Shawnees. The white American's retaliation, however, was severe. Their army destroyed many Shawnee villages. Hoping to starve the Indians, the soldiers always made certain to ruin the villagers' food reserves.

In 1795, Indian leaders from numerous tribes, including the Shawnee, met with American officials in Greenville, Ohio, to sign a peace treaty. Known as the

INDIAN LEADERS FORM NUMEROUS TRIBES SIGNED
THE TREATY OF GREENVILLE. THIS UNFAIR AGREEMENT COST
THE SHAWNEES AND OTHER INDIANS MUCH OF THEIR LAND.

Treaty of Greenville, the agreement was difficult for the American Indians to accept. As might be expected, the Indians were forced to give up a great deal of land, much of it being Shawnee territory. As the Indians' losses had been great, they felt they had few choices. Ninety-one chiefs from various tribes signed the treaty, including Blue Jacket and other Shawnee leaders.

Yet one outstanding Shawnee chief was not at Greenville. He had refused to sign that treaty or any other. Experience had taught him that the whites never kept their word. His name was Tecumseh. He was a Shawnee leader whom the Indians respected and the whites would fear.

TECUMSEH

Tecumseh may have been the Shawnee's most brilliant and renowned leader. His father, Pucksinwah, was the respected war chief who turned his adopted white son Blue Jacket into a leader as well. Tecumseh was well known for his bravery and winning battle strategies. He was also an outstanding speaker who readily inspired others.

Throughout his life, this energetic war chief warned his people against giving in to the whites' demands. He refused to sign the Treaty of Greenville and urged other Shawnee leaders not to do so. Tecumseh later broke with those Shawnees he believed had fallen victim to the whites' lust for power and land. He and his followers left to begin a new village of their own, away from the encroaching whites.

Among those who went with Tecumseh was his younger brother Tenskwatawa. Unlike Tecumseh,

SHAWNEE LEADER TECUMSEH'S BRILLIANCE
AND BRAVERY HAS INSPIRED A NUMBER OF
CURRENT BOOKS AND FILMS ABOUT HIS LIFE.

TENSKWATAWA,
TECUMSEH'S YOUNGER
BROTHER

Tenskwatawa had not seemed very promising as a child. It was important for young Shawnee males to be good hunters and fighters, but Tenskwatawa was neither. As a child, he had lost an eye in a hunting accident. Later as a young adult, he spent most of his time drinking whiskey.

But in 1805, Tenskwatawa's life changed forever. He fell into a coma from which he was not expected to recover. His family had even begun making his funeral arrangements. But to everyone's surprise, he came to claiming that he had died and returned to life. Tenskwatawa said that while in the spirit world, he saw how to drive the whites away. He strongly urged all American Indians to reject white customs and return to their peoples' ancient ways.

Tenskwatawa's message spread. Meanwhile his older brother Tecumseh had been actively addressing American Indians as well. Tecumseh traveled throughout the region asking the various tribes to unite against the whites. He felt that unless all American Indians acted as a single force, there was no hope of keeping whatever land or dignity they had left.

White officials were wary of Tecumseh. They saw him as an effective leader capable of attracting followers from various tribes. But they had other plans for the Indians.

Now the white government wanted American Indians to stop hunting and gathering their food and instead farm small plots of land. If the Indians cooperated, the government hoped, the whites could eventually take over much of the remaining land without a struggle. While some Shawnees went along with the whites' scheme, Tecumseh flatly refused. He often claimed that he would rather be dead than live like a white man. He watched sadly as many of his people failed as homesteaders, went into debt, and eventually became dependent on meager government handouts.

Among the whites who were especially anxious to bring Tecumseh down was then–Indian Territory governor William Henry Harrison. Harrison, who later became a U.S. president, tried to convince various American Indian chiefs that selling their peoples' land to the whites would be best for their tribes. But Tecumseh was outspoken about Harrison's trickery. The Shawnee war chief repeatedly argued that the whites already had too much American Indian land. He further stressed that Harrison's treaties were invalid and urged American Indians not to abide by them. Although Harrison and Tecumseh met on several occasions to try to resolve their differences, they were unable to do so. The men remained bitter enemies to the end.

TECUMSEH ANGRILY ACCUSED INDIAN TERRITORY
GOVERNOR WILLIAM HENRY HARRISON; THE FAMOUS
SHAWNEE LEADER DIED ON THE BATTLEFIELD THAT DAY.

CHIEF BLACK HOOF (SHOWN HERE) NAIVELY URGED THE
SHAWNEES TO GO ALONG WITH THE WHITES' PLAN FOR THEM
TO BECOME FARMERS. UNFORTUNATELY, HIS FOLLOWERS
NEVER RECEIVED THE TOOLS OR TRAINING PROMISED THEM.

Meanwhile, Tecumseh's village known as Prophetstown continued to attract new followers. American Indians from numerous tribes who agreed with Tecumseh joined him there. But in November 1811, the situation soured for the Indians. That fall, Tecumseh had traveled south hoping to win the support of some of the larger tribes. Aware that the Shawnees' outstanding war chief was away, Harrison quickly amassed his military forces and prepared to attack.

During Tecumseh's absence, Tenskwatawa was left in charge. Unfortunately, he lacked his brother's leadership and warfare skills. Although Tecumseh had warned him to flee if the white soldiers approached, Tenskwatawa decided to attack the whites before Harrison's men reached the village.

The American Indians suffered a serious defeat that day. Tenskwatawa stood on a hill above the battleground promising to render magically the whites' weapons useless. While Harrison remained at the battlesite directing his men, before long Tenskwatawa was nowhere to be found. Much of Tecumseh's fighting force was lost that day and the white soldiers went on to destroy Prophetstown. Tenskwatawa was later captured by the Indians he had deserted in battle. Although he was not killed for his cowardice, he was no longer admired and respected as a Shawnee prophet.

Tecumseh worked hard to rebuild a united Indian front, but his brother's errors hurt his efforts. Nevertheless, after a while, Tecumseh and his fighters again posed a serious threat to area white settlements. He even managed to ally his forces with the British in Canada.

The British were once again at war with the white Americans in the conflict known as the War of 1812. The British reasoned that the white Americans' defeat would benefit both the Indians and themselves. And while Tecumseh had not liked how the British treated the Shawnees in the past, he now needed them to help halt the white American expansion.

Although the British and Indian forces were somewhat successful, the white Americans were more so. On October 5, 1813, they fought Indian and British soldiers at the Battle of the Thames. After a number of their men were killed, the British hastily retreated. But despite the battle's tide and their loss of men, the Indians fought on.

Tecumseh was among those who died that day on the battlefield. The night before he had predicted that he would be killed. Sadly, he was right, just, as he had been right about the whites' true intentions toward his people. Today he is remembered as an outstanding and courageous American Indian leader.

HERE AT THE BATTLE OF THE THAMES, INDIAN AND BRITISH
FORCES FOUGHT THE AMERICANS. IT WAS THE LAST
TIME TECUMSEH WOULD FACE HIS OLD ENEMY WILLIAM
HENRY HARRISON—THE FAMOUS SHAWNEE LEADER DIED
ON THE BATTLEFIELD THAT DAY.

MODERN DAY SHAWNEE

Following Tecumseh's death, the Shawnees' plight, as well as that of other Indians, worsened. The Shawnees never again knew the freedom they had had before the whites' arrival. After Britain's defeat in the War of 1812, the Shawnees and other tribes were forced to sell yet another large portion of their acreage to the whites for an extremely low price.

As before the War of 1812, the Shawnees remained divided among several factions (groups). Through the years, these groups sometimes relocated for various reasons. The government, however, eventually removed the Shawnees to reservations in Oklahoma. Today, these American Indians exist in three distinctly separate tribes known as the Absentee Shawnees, the Eastern Shawnees, and the Loyal, or Cherokee, Shawnees.

These Shawnees live in modern housing and many have professions or jobs in mainstream society.

IN THIS 1974 PHOTO,
ABSENTEE SHAWNEES DISPLAY THEIR
RECENTLY DESIGNED TRIBAL FLAG.

MODERN-DAY SHAWNEE HAVE TAUGHT
THEIR YOUNG PEOPLE TRADITIONAL
BEAD AND RIBBON WORK

Yet all three Shawnee tribes have tried in some ways
to keep their ancient culture alive. Often this has
meant continuing rituals and ceremonies such as the
War Dance and the Spring and Fall Bread Dances.
The Absentee Shawnees have been particularly active
in preserving their past. They have offered young
people a chance to learn the Shawnee language and
made sure that their people's bead and ribbon work
has continued.

Shawnee chiefs still oversee ceremonies and rituals. But present-day Shawnee tribes have tribal business councils to decide on matters affecting the group. As in the past, Shawnee women often hold positions of importance within their tribes.

The Shawnees are a strong and resourceful people. Despite various tribal divisions at different times in history, they survived. Their spirit and determination continues today.

THESE SHAWNEE CHILDREN LOOK FORWARD TO A BRIGHT FUTURE.

GLOSSARY

Annual yearly

Captive a person who has been taken and held as a prisoner

Deity a god

Fast to go purposely without food for a period of time

Game hunted wild animals or birds

Moccasins soft leather shoes that were worn by the Shawnees and other Indians

Msikamelwi the large wooden structure at the center of a Shawnee village that served as a council house and a community center

Prophecy a prediction about the future

Reservation a tract of land set aside by the government for Indian use

Ritual a religious ceremony or rite

Shaman an American Indian healer believed to have spiritual powers

Tanned the process through which an animal hide or skin is turned into leather

Treaty an agreement between nations or groups of people

Tribute money or goods given by one nation or group of people to another in return for the promise of peace or protection

Wegiwa a Shawnee home with a frame made of wooden poles covered with tree bark or animal skins

Vision quest the practice of a young Indian who, having fasted, goes off to a remote place hoping to see his or her spirit guide in a dream or vision. The Indians believed that a person's spirit guide protected that individual from danger and harm.

FOR FURTHER READING

Bruchac, Joseph. *Thirteen Moons on a Turtle's Back: A Native American Year of Moons.* New York: Philomel Books, 1992.

Connell, Kate. *These Lands Are Ours: Tecumseh's Fight for the Old Northwest.* Austin, TX: Raintree Steck-Vaughn, 1993.

Hirschfelder, Arlene B., and Beverly R. Singer. *Rising Voices: Writing of Young Native Americans.* New York: Scribner & Sons, 1992.

Kent, Zachary. *Tecumseh: Shawnee Chief.* Chicago: Children's Press, 1992.

Maestro, Betsy. *Exploration and Conquest: The Americans After Columbus.* New York: Lothrop, Lee & Shepard, 1994.

Monroe, Jean Guard. *First Houses: Native American Homes and Sacred Structures*. Boston: Houghton Mifflin, 1993.

O'Neill, Laurie. *The Shawnees: People of the Eastern Woodlands*. Brookfield, CT: Millbrook Press, 1995.

Shorto, Russell. *Tecumseh and the Dream of an American Indian Nation*. Englewood Cliffs, NJ: Silver Burdett, 1989.

INDEX

Popular author Elaine Landau worked as a newspaper reporter, an editor, and a youth services librarian before becoming a full-time writer. She has written more than ninety nonfiction books for young people, including *The Sioux*, *The Hopi*, *The Cherokees*, *The Chilula*, and *The Pomo*. Ms. Landau, who has a bachelor's degree in English and journalism from New York University and a master's degree in library and information science from Pratt Institute, lives in New Jersey with her husband and son.